SMALL FLAMES

ZURI THE GOLDEN DRAGON

A.M. LUZZADER

ILLUSTRATED BY
JOSHUA BOSTWICK

Published by Knowledge Forest Press
P.O. Box 6331
Logan, UT 84341

Ebook ISBN-13: 978-1-949078-88-6
Paperback ISBN-13: 978-1-949078-87-9

Cover design by BookCoverZone

Editing by Chadd VanZanten

Interior illustrations by Joshua Bostwick

For Layla

ONE

Zuri stepped out of her cavern and onto the steep mountainside where she lived with her grandmother. After taking a deep breath of mountain air, Zuri smiled. It was a bright, beautiful morning in the Dragon Realm of Savra. The sun shone in the sky. Birds chirped and water roared softly in the river far below.

Zuri was a young golden dragon. She was only ten years old, but she already knew how to fight well, and she was covered in an armor of tough scales. She was large and strong for her age. Because Zuri was a golden dragon, her wings and scales were golden. They sparkled brightly in the morning light.

Many kinds of dragons dwelled in the Realm of

Savra. Each had different skills and abilities. Gold, red, and orange dragons were large and powerful. They were known as "hot dragons" because they breathed fire, lava, and molten gold.

Dragons who were purple, white, and silver breathed ice, snow, and freezing wind. These were known as "cold dragons" and they were small and slender, but very quick.

Black dragons breathed acid and were known to be great leaders. Brown dragons breathed mud and were known for their building skills. There were many other dragon kinds, too.

On any other morning, Zuri would be on her way to classes. She had been training for years to be a Valor Dragon. The Valor Dragons were the protectors of the Realm of Savra. They were the soldiers and guards and fighters who guarded the dragon lands from danger.

Zuri and many other dragons of her age had training classes almost every day. They learned how to fight and fly. They learned how to be soldiers and guards.

But today, there was no training. That's because Zuri had graduated!

The first part of Zuri's Valor Dragon training

was over. She was now a member of the Small Flames. The Small Flames were young dragons who were almost ready to be Valor Dragons.

All Zuri had to do now was compete in the Fire Ridge Tournament, where the Small Flames fought with each other. They fought one-on-one in the arenas at Fire Ridge. Those who fought well would be invited to become Valor Dragons.

The word "valor" means "bravery and boldness when facing great danger." The Valor Dragons were the bravest and boldest dragons in the Realm of Savra. Zuri admired the Valor Dragons very much because they put their lives at risk to keep the rest of the dragons safe. She also admired them because both of her parents had been Valor Dragons. Zuri's mother's name was Kyra the Yellow. Her father's name was Raxo the Brown.

Zuri's grandmother Ashti came out of the cavern and stood by Zuri's side. Ashti was a green dragon. She was quite old, with deep wrinkles around her eyes and neck. Ashti did not walk very quickly, and she hardly ever flew anymore. Zuri loved her very much. Ashti was Kyra's mother and Zuri's grandmother.

"There's my golden girl," Ashti said to Zuri.

"Good morning, Grandma!" said Zuri. Ashti was more like a mother to Zuri, instead of a grandmother. "Isn't it a lovely morning?"

"Yes, but I'm surprised you're awake," said Ashti. "I thought you might sleep in, now that you don't have classes."

"I couldn't sleep," said Zuri. "I can't stop thinking about the Fire Ridge Tournament."

"I thought so," said Ashti. "Just like your mother. When she first became a Small Flame, she didn't sleep much, either."

"Was my mother afraid?" asked Zuri. "Was she afraid of fighting in the tournament?"

"Oh, maybe a little," said Ashti. "I think most dragons are a little nervous about the tournament."

Zuri didn't remember much about her parents. They had gone away to war when Zuri was just a hatchling. Ashti and other dragon mothers had raised and taken care of Zuri.

The tales Zuri heard about her mother Kyra were very inspiring. Kyra had completed her Valor Dragon training with perfect scores. She competed at Fire Ridge without losing a single fight. Kyra never even lost a practice fight!

When Kyra was a grown dragon, she fought the

shadow vultures in the Crooked Sky Wars. The shadow vultures hated dragons. They tried to take over the Realm of Savra by stealing the souls of dragons.

During the wars, Kyra was a major in the Valor Dragons. She led her troops into battle and won many victories. It was said she once fought ten shadow vultures by herself, and won!

Sadly, Kyra was killed during the Crooked Sky

Wars during a sneak attack by the shadow vultures. Zuri was only a baby dragon when it happened, but she still felt sad about it sometimes.

Even though Kyra was gone, she would always be considered one of the greatest Valor Dragons in the Realm of Savra.

Zuri tried to chase away her feelings of fear and anxiety.

My mother was never nervous or fearful, thought Zuri. *She was brave. I must be like her. I must never fear.*

Zuri's father, Raxo, also fought in the Crooked Sky Wars, and he was also brave and skillful. He once saved his entire squad from capture by inspiring them to fight back when they were greatly outnumbered.

But no one knew what happened to Raxo after the wars. He simply disappeared. Some said he was also killed. Others said that Raxo's heart was so broken by Kyra's death, he wandered out into the wastes and was never seen again.

And so Ashti raised her granddaughter Zuri as if she were her own hatchling. Zuri had lived with Ashti for most of her life. It was a little different from other dragon families. However, Zuri couldn't imagine any other way.

Ashti noticed Zuri staring at Fire Ridge. It was a mountain in the center of the Savra Realm, where the great dragon arenas were located. It was where Zuri would fight to become a Valor Dragon. There were many arenas at Fire Ridge. Each was surrounded by stadiums with benches so that dragons from all over the realm could watch the tournament fights.

Ashti knew Zuri must be thinking of the tournament, which would begin soon.

"Zuri," said Ashti, "if you win your tournament fights, I will be so proud of you. But if you *don't* win, I will *still* be so proud of you! You are my golden girl. You shine in everything you do."

Zuri wanted Ashti to be proud of her. There were many dragon mothers who helped raise Zuri. She wanted them to be proud, too. Zuri even sometimes thought her father might return one day and tell Zuri that he was proud of her. She would be happy to make them all proud by becoming a Valor Dragon.

Zuri also wished to become a Valor Dragon so that she could help other dragons and protect the Realm of Savra. She wanted to keep the realm safe from danger.

However, deep down, Zuri wanted most of all to be like her mother, and she wanted to make her mother proud. Zuri knew her mother had been killed in the Crooked Sky Wars. But Zuri often wondered if Kyra could see her, and if she was proud. Kyra had been brave, skilled, tough, and valorous. She was the perfect Valor Dragon. Zuri wanted to be that way, too. She wanted to be one of the greatest Valor Dragons, just as her mother had been.

CHAPTER
TWO

Soon it was time for Zuri to report to Fire Ridge. She had graduated from the first part of her Valor Dragon training with perfect scores, just like her mother. She was a Small Flame, just as her mother had been.

Now she must go to the arenas at Fire Ridge for two weeks of practice fights. Every day for two weeks, Zuri and her classmates would fight each other to improve their skills and abilities.

"But I will never be defeated," Zuri told herself. "Just like my mother."

As a group, Zuri and her classmates were known as a "clutch." Zuri and her clutch trained and studied together for years. There were about thirty of them. Now they would go to Fire Ridge to fight each other. But these weren't ordinary fights. Most fights are nasty and mean. Most fights are also hateful and quite pointless.

The fights at Fire Ridge were different. They were more like competitions, such as when you play chess or soccer. Each Small Flame wanted to win, of course. However, the Small Flames did not hate each other. They did not fight because of anger. The Small Flames fought with respect and friendship. The fights were meant to find out who should be invited to be Valor Dragons.

Zuri's clutch was trained by Master Rahu, another one of the great Valor Dragons. He was a massive red dragon and covered in sharp, hard scales that flashed like flakes of red steel. His shoulders and legs were large and muscular. His teeth and talons were long and razor-sharp. Master Rahu's voice was as deep and booming as thunder. It was said that no one could survive a strike from the huge horns on his head, nor a strike from his powerful tail.

Master Rahu knew Zuri's mother. He had fought beside her in the Crooked Sky Wars.

On the very first day that Zuri arrived at Fire Ridge, Master Rahu told the Small Flames to gather in the main arena. When they had done so, Master Rahu told them all to pick a partner and have a practice fight.

At first Zuri looked around for Enzo. He was a red dragon and a great fighter, but he was already practice-fighting with his best friend, Ajax, another red dragon. Then Zuri spotted Stak, a black dragon. Stak was also a very good fighter. He was covered in hard scales, and he knew how to breathe acid.

"Stak!" cried Zuri. "Will you fight?"

"I will fight," replied Stak.

Zuri and Stak found an open area on the far side of the arena. Zuri got very excited to fight.

Stak started the battle by breathing a stream of toxic acid at Zuri. However, Zuri knew the acid would not damage her golden scales at first. So, she turned the acid away by blocking it with one wing. Then she rushed in close to Stak and gave him a hard tail strike to the neck. While Stak was still stunned, Zuri leaped onto Stak's back and pinned his wings to the floor of the arena. She used her molten gold breath to help hold him down.

"I yield!" cried Stak. "I give up!"

Zuri said, "Thank you for a good fight my friend! You have my respect!"

Zuri was not surprised that she had won the fight. Just like her mother Kyra, Zuri had never been defeated in a practice fight.

"And you have my respect," replied Stak, rubbing his bruised neck. "Wow, you've got a really powerful tail!"

"Thanks, Stak!" said Zuri. "See you around!"

The Small Flames fought with each other, and they had competed for the best grades in classes. However, they also played games and ate meals together. The Small Flames always stayed friends and they respected each other.

Zuri quickly found another Small Flame to fight. Her name was Ryri. She was a silver dragon who breathed super-cold air. Zuri knew if she was hit by Ryri's cold breath, it would cool off the molten lead in her belly. If that happened, Zuri would not be able to use her breath weapon.

Ryri struck first by unleashing her freezing wind breath, but Zuri was simply too fast. She darted to the right, and the cold air whooshed past her harmlessly. Zuri again used her quick, powerful tail to strike back. Ryri was knocked back. She rolled and tumbled into the sand of the arena.

Now it was Zuri's turn to use her breath weapon. She roared out a stream of hot liquid gold, which burned and weakened Ryri. The silver dragon tried to escape the gold by flying up, but Zuri flew up to meet her and slammed her back down.

"I yield! I yield!" groaned Ryri. She was already covered with burns and bruises.

All these injuries and burns might sound harsh, but the dragons of Savra were very, very tough. Even young dragons were used to fighting hard, and they healed quickly.

"Thank you for a great fight, Ryri!" called Zuri. "You have my respect!"

"Same to you, Zuri," Ryri called back, nursing her injuries.

Zuri had beaten two opponents in almost no time.

This is easy! thought Zuri. *But I guess that's how it will be for me. My mother never lost a fight, and neither will I!*

She looked around for another opponent and spotted Rog the Brown. But Rog had just been defeated, and he was heading for the edge of the arena to rest. Zuri galloped and soared around the arena, but she could not find another fighting partner.

Just then, Master Rahu flew into the air and shouted, "Small Flames, stop! Fighting practice is over! Very good! You all fought well! Now, circle up." His voice boomed across the arena.

All the Small Flames sat in a circle around Master Rahu. He gave them some advice and wisdom. He took a few questions, and then dismissed the Small Flames to eat and rest.

The practice fights would continue for two whole

weeks. Zuri felt very excited. She had won her first two practice fights, and she just knew she would never lose.

"I can practice-fight all day long for the next two weeks," she said to herself. "No one can defeat me."

CHAPTER

THREE

The Fire Ridge Tournament was a special time in the Dragon Realm of Savra. You might say it was the dragon holiday season. Dragons traveled long distances to Fire Ridge for the special events. There were holiday foods to eat, such as brimstone pie. There were hot oils to drink with different flavors. Many Valor Dragons came to demonstrate their fighting and flying abilities. They even gave each other gifts.

The most interesting events, of course, were the Fire Ridge fights, where the Small Flames competed to become Valor Dragons. Everyone in the realm wanted to see the fights. They wanted to know who the newest Valor Dragons would be. And so, at every fight, the stadiums were packed with dragons of all kinds and all ages. They cheered for their favorite Small Flames. They cheered for their family members and friends.

However, the Fire Ridge Tournament hadn't started yet. First came two weeks of preparation for the Small Flames. They couldn't just start fighting each other as soon as they graduated. They needed to practice first.

Before Zuri had gone to Fire Ridge to begin the practice fighting, she spent a lot of time looking at a painting of her mother, Kyra. It hung on a wall in the main cave of the cavern where Zuri lived with her Grandma Ashti.

"You look just like your mother when she was your age," Ashti said to Zuri.

There were other grown-up dragons who had known Kyra, and they told Zuri the same thing.

"Doesn't she look just like Kyra?" they said. "Yes, it's quite uncanny."

This made Zuri smile. Kyra was a very beautiful dragon. However, Zuri hoped that she got more than just her mother's looks. She hoped that she had also gained the flying and combat skills she would need to become a Valor Dragon.

Indeed, Zuri fought well in the practice fights. Her flying skills were amazing. Her fighting skills were even better. And she was really learning a lot about her breath weapon. As a golden dragon, Zuri breathed out a stream of melted, liquid gold. It was extremely hot, and it was good at burning her opponents. However, during the practice fights, she learned that she could also use it in different ways.

For example, if she shot out her gold just right, she could form it into sharp golden missiles or heavy golden cannonballs. This made her feel even more powerful and more difficult to defeat.

Soon the two weeks of practice fighting came to an end. Master Rahu gathered them together for one final talk.

"Small Flames," he said, "the tournament begins tomorrow. No more practice! Tomorrow you will compete in the actual tournament."

Master Rahu had already told the Small Flames several times that they would have to do more than win their fights. He told them that a group of dragons called the Valor Judges would be watching them during the tournaments. It was the Valor Judges who would decide which Small Flames would be invited to be Valor Dragons.

"These judges will look for more than simple victory or defeat," Master Rahu reminded them. "They will watch all of you Small Flames to see what kind of dragons you are."

The Small Flames nodded their heads.

"What kind of things do you think the Valor Judges will be looking for while you fight in the tournament?" asked Master Rahu.

Zuri raised her paw.

"Yes, Zuri?" said Master Rahu.

"Perfect fighting ability!" she said with a big smile.

Master Rahu narrowed his eyes. "Maybe," he said. "However, not many of us can fight perfectly all the time."

A Small Flame named Sarc raised his paw.

"Yes, Sarc? What do you think?" said Master Rahu.

"Will the judges be watching for Small Flames who show respect and act with honor?" asked Sarc.

"Yes!" said Master Rahu. "They will be looking for exactly that!"

Zuri raised her paw again.

"Zuri?" said Master Rahu. "Do you have another answer?"

"Won't the Valor Judges choose the Small Flames who have the best combat skills?" she asked.

"Of course," said Master Rahu. "But fighting and flying skills are not enough. Let's say we simply allowed all the Small Flames to fight each other. Then we dismissed all the losers and invited all the winners to be Valor Dragons. What would happen?"

"Only the very best fighters would be chosen to be Valor Dragons," replied Zuri.

"Exactly," said Master Rahu. "That would not be good."

"Huh?" said Zuri.

Master Rahu continued. "It is good to have Valor Dragons that are very good at fighting, but they must also be respectful, kind, understanding, and brave. They must be good planners. They must be good leaders. They must even be good followers."

Zuri thought about this. It still didn't make sense. She raised her paw again.

"Yes, Zuri?" said Master Rahu. "You have another question?"

Zuri frowned and said, "So, I can win every single practice fight, and every single tournament fight, and still not be invited to be a Valor Dragon?"

"That's a good question," said Master Rahu. "If you win every single tournament fight the judges give you, you will probably be invited to be a Valor Dragon."

Zuri smiled. She planned on never losing a single fight.

But Master Rahu raised one talon of his big paw. "However," he added, "you might win all your fights and *not* be invited to be a Valor Dragon. It has happened before. It all depends on what *the judges* see in you. Valor Dragons must be more than great fighters. Otherwise, we would simply call them 'Fighter Dragons'."

Zuri blinked as though she didn't understand.

"Does that answer your question?" asked Master Rahu.

Zuri nodded and said, "Yes, Master Rahu," but she was struggling to understand. It didn't seem right.

I am the best fighting Small Flame in this whole clutch, she thought. *I might even be the best fighting Small Flame in the entire realm. I'm just like my mother. I fight perfectly. I fly perfectly. But if I win every fight, I still might not be a Valor Dragon. That's not fair!*

What was she supposed to do now?

These thoughts kept Zuri up all night. The sleeping caves and beds at Fire Ridge were full of sharp, pointy rocks—very comfortable for Small Flames. However, even though the rocks were sharp and jagged, Zuri could not sleep. She had perfected her fighting ability, but now she was afraid of being eliminated for some other reason. When the sun peeked into her sleeping cave in the morning, she had not slept at all.

FOUR

Z<small>URI REPORTED TO THE DINING CAVE FOR BREAKFAST,</small> but she couldn't eat anything. She was too drowsy. She hadn't been able to sleep all night, but now she felt like she could lie down on the dining table and sleep all day.

"I have been fighting nine or ten times every day for the past two weeks," Zuri mumbled to herself. "All I have to do today is win one fight, and then I'll be able to rest. No one can beat me. This will be no problem."

After breakfast, Master Rahu took the Small Flames to a large cavern deep inside Fire Ridge. Here they would wait until a judge called them up to the arena.

There were many Small Flames of all kinds in the waiting caverns. There were reds, goldens, and oranges—hot dragons from the south. There were silvers, whites, and purples from the north. They had come from all over Savra Realm to compete to be Valor Dragons.

Zuri took a seat and waited. An hour went by, and then another. Zuri was so tired, she dozed off and awoke only when she heard her name called.

A judge entered the cavern and said, "Zuri the Golden, report to the arena."

Zuri blinked the sleep from her eyes and shook the cobwebs from her mind. It was time. She arose and hurried to the arena gate. A Valor Judge told her where to stand.

But then the judge took a closer look at Zuri and asked, "Are you quite all right, Small Flame? Is something wrong with you?"

"No, ma'am," said Zuri. "I just didn't sleep well last night."

"Hmm," said the judge. "It is your duty to be well-rested for the tournament. I hope you are ready to fight."

"I am," replied Zuri. "At least I hope I am," she mumbled to herself.

The arena gate opened. The sun poured into the hallway and Zuri squinted. She heard the roar of the dragons seated in the stadium. They were cheering for another fight.

Zuri stepped out into the arena. A Small Flame was entering the arena from the other side. They met in the center.

"I am Obok!" said Zuri's opponent. His voice was deep and loud.

He was a huge red dragon. He was only ten

years old, like Zuri, but he seemed like he was nearly the size of Master Rahu. He looked very strong, but he was also quick on his feet. Obok spread his wings and flapped them a few times. Even though he flapped them slowly, he raised a big cloud of sand and dust from the arena floor.

Zuri was large for her age, too, but she was much smaller than Obok. She stared up at him. He looked like a small mountain who happened to be covered in red scales.

A referee was in the arena to enforce the rules and make sure the Small Flames fought fairly. She was a slender purple dragon.

"You shall fight until one yields," the referee said in a loud voice, "or until one of you is unable to continue fighting."

Zuri and Obok nodded.

"You must fight fairly!" called the referee. "No attacks to the eyes, no bites to the neck, and no hidden weapons. Understand?"

Zuri and Obok nodded again.

"Good! Now, touch paws and take your starting positions," said the referee.

Zuri and Obok returned to their starting positions on opposite sides of the arena.

Then the referee waved her black flag, and the fight began!

Obok was very large, but he moved with great speed. Before Zuri knew it, Obok had flown low and fast across the arena. Obok had his head down and was going to ram Zuri with his mighty horns. Zuri dodged to the left, but she still had sleep in her bones. She moved a little too slowly. Obok's head and horns slammed into Zuri's chest, and she was flung back into the arena wall.

"Urmf!" grunted Zuri.

She'd never been hit so hard! Her whole right side went numb. She couldn't even move her right wing! Instead of trying to fly, she shot Obok with several gold missiles. They were sharp and fast, but Zuri was still slightly groggy, and she missed.

Obok turned and attacked again, launching his fierce breath weapon. Zuri was engulfed in fire! She had no idea the breath weapon of a Small Flame could be so strong. It was like a hurricane of flames! Zuri returned the attack by breathing her stream of molten gold at Obok. But it was no use. Obok's breath weapon simply blasted her gold into vapor.

Now Obok beat his wings and rose into the air.

He was a massive dragon, but he lifted from the arena floor quite gracefully. The dust he rose made it hard for Zuri to see him. She squinted up through the glare of the sun and the swirling dust, but she couldn't see Obok.

Then, from out of nowhere, Obok struck Zuri from behind.

Zuri was knocked out cold and thrown into the sand of the arena.

"The fight is over!" cried the referee. "The fight is over! The winner is Obok the Red!"

CHAPTER
FIVE

ZURI AWOKE A SHORT TIME LATER AND SLOWLY opened her eyes. She blinked a little. Then she squinted. After a while, she saw Master Rahu standing over her. She was in a large cave, lying on her back.

Her back hurt.

Her front hurt.

Both sides of her were hurting.

"How are you feeling, Zuri?" asked Master Rahu.

"W—where am I?" she said. Her voice was soft and scratchy. She looked around and found herself on a comfortable bed of jagged rocks.

There were other Small Flames on other beds. Some of them moaned and groaned with pain.

"You're in the medical cave," said Master Rahu.

"Why?" she asked. "Is someone hurt?"

"You got hit pretty hard by Obok the Red," said Master Rahu. "You don't remember?"

Zuri blinked. "I—I lost? I lost my first tournament fight?"

"Yes," said Master Rahu. "But—"

"Oh, no!" Zuri shouted as she sat up on the bed. "I've been eliminated! What would my mother think?" She began to cry.

"Whoa, whoa!" said Master Rahu. He patted Zuri on the back—but not too hard. She was covered with bruises and burns. "You were not eliminated, Zuri!"

Zuri stopped her crying and looked at Master Rahu. "I wasn't eliminated? Why not? I thought you said I lost!"

"Zuri," said Master Rahu. "Don't you remember what we talked about just yesterday? It's not always just about winning or losing fights! The judges have been watching you practice. They watched you fight. I guess they think you deserve another fight. Or maybe two. Or three! You never know."

"I'm not eliminated?" Zuri asked.

"No," said Master Rahu.

"Are you sure?"

"Yes, Zuri," said Master Rahu. "You're still in the tournament. However, I thought you might be eliminated. What happened out there? I've never seen you fight so slowly. It was as if your feet were stuck in lava porridge!"

Zuri sighed and said, "I didn't sleep last night. I

was so worried about fighting perfectly, I stayed up all night."

"I see," said Master Rahu. "Well, that explains it. Zuri, I think you are being too hard on yourself. No one must be perfect or fight perfectly. You must only do your best. You are an excellent fighter. Next time you fight, just go out there with no expectations, and let the fight happen."

"Okay, Master Rahu," replied Zuri. "I'll try."

"Why don't you come up to my seat at the arena and watch a few of the fights," said Master Rahu. "Some of your clutch mates are there. Then you can go to your cave and have a good night's rest."

They went up to the main arena. Zuri saw her friends Maji and Husha fight. Then she saw Jory fight. Jory was a small orange dragon. He was always a little slower and weaker than the other dragons in their Small Flames clutch. But Jory won!

"If Jory won," Zuri grumbled to herself, "I should be winning, too!"

Then Zuri thought about what Master Rahu had said. He told her that she shouldn't worry about fighting perfectly.

Master Rahu said something like, "Just let the fight happen."

No! thought Zuri. *I can't just "let the fight happen." I must fight with all my skill! There are some very strong, tough, and huge fighters here. Obok was huge and very skilled. If I am to win, and if I am to become a Valor Dragon, I must fight perfectly!*

CHAPTER
SIX

AFTER HER LOSS IN THE FIRE RIDGE TOURNAMENT, Zuri was given three days to rest, heal, and recover her strength. However, instead of resting in bed or watching more of the tournament fights, Zuri flew home.

Her grandmother Ashti had gotten too old to fly all the way to Fire Ridge, so she had stayed at home while Zuri went to the tournament. Ashti was very happy to see Zuri.

"Zuri!" said Ashti when Zuri came into the cavern. Then she got a closer look at Zuri. "Oh, no! Look at your cuts and bruises!"

"I'm all right, Grandma," said Zuri with a sad smile.

"Well, what are you doing at home?" asked Ashti. "Shouldn't you be fighting in the arenas?"

"I fought yesterday," Zuri replied, her head hanging low. "And I lost."

"Yes, my dear," said her grandmother. "I heard that you lost. But that's all right. Everyone is still so proud of you."

"Thank you, Grandma," said Zuri, but her voice sounded sad.

"Does this mean you've been eliminated?" asked Ashti. "Is that why you're home so soon?"

"No," Zuri answered. "I haven't been eliminated. I have another fight in three days."

"Well, then," said Ashti, "everything will be all right! Losing is not so bad if you're not eliminated. Besides, every dragon must lose a fight now and then."

"My mother never lost any fights," said Zuri. "She would not be proud of me if she saw me fight so poorly."

"Whatever do you mean?" asked Ashti.

"I mean I fought like a total beginner!" said Zuri.

"No, no, no," said Ashti. "What do you mean your *mother never lost any fights*?"

"Well, she never did," replied Zuri, shrugging

her shoulders. "In her Small Flames training, in her practice fights, and during her tournament fights, she never lost!"

"Who told you *that?*" asked Ashti with a puzzled look on her face.

Now it was Zuri's turn to be puzzled. "Hmm. I don't know exactly who told me. That's just what I heard at Valor Dragon training from the other Small Flames and from my teachers."

"Zuri, dear," said Ashti softly, "I think those must be rumors. Kyra lost *several* fights."

"What?" cried Zuri, her eyes suddenly wide.

"Yes, of course," said Ashti. "Kyra lost practice fights and she even lost a fight during her Small Flames tournament. I was much younger in those days, of course, and I flew with her to Fire Ridge. I watched all her practice fights. I watched her fight in the tournament. Kyra always fought beautifully, but she lost sometimes, too."

When Zuri heard this, she had to sit down.

"I remember her practice-fight with Garr the Black!" said Ashti.

"Kyra fought *Garr?*" said Zuri, amazed. "*The* Garr the Black? *Supreme General* Garr?"

"Yes," said Ashti. "They were in the same clutch.

And it was only a practice fight. Oh, but he was enormous, and what a breath weapon!"

"What happened?" cried Zuri.

"Ah, what a fight it was!" said Ashti, "As soon as it started, Garr faked left, you see, and caught your mother off-guard. He was very clever."

Zuri watched as Ashti acted out the fight with her paws.

"Kyra thought Garr was coming in for a tail

strike," said Ashti, her voice high and excited, "but he jumped to the right and shot Kyra with his acid. She was blinded for a few seconds. After that, the fight was over very quickly. They stayed friends, of course, and later worked together as Valor Dragons."

Zuri couldn't believe what she was hearing! She didn't know whether to be upset or relieved.

"Why are you so shocked, dear?" asked Ashti. She came to Zuri's side.

"All this time I thought my mom had never been defeated," Zuri replied. "Why would everyone tell me that?"

"It's quite understandable, my dear," said Ashti. She patted Zuri's cheek. "You see, your mother really was one of the greatest Valor Dragons. She was wise, brave, kind, and a magnificent dragon fighter. Everyone admired her."

"Yes, I know," said Zuri.

"Well," Ashti continued, "when everyone looks up to a dragon like Kyra, rumors get started. We remember certain dragons as bigger and better and greater than they were in real life. I think rumors have turned Kyra from a real-life hero into a story-book legend."

"But why?" asked Zuri.

Ashti thought about this. "Maybe it's a way for us to hold on to our respect for those we love. Maybe it's something we do to make sure no one will ever forget them."

"Interesting," said Zuri.

"It's just an exaggeration," said Ashti. "And it's really just a *little* exaggeration if you think about it. Kyra was not undefeated, but she only lost a *few* fights."

"So, she lost a *tournament* fight?" asked Zuri.

"Yes, that's right," said Ashti with a nod of her head. "She lost to a clever green dragon named Tran. In fact, she lost her *very first* tournament fight— just like you!"

"Wow," said Zuri, putting a paw on her forehead.

"Your mother was so nervous on the night before her first fight, she couldn't sleep," Ashti explained. "The poor dear went to her fight almost too sleepy to hold her head up."

"That's what happened to me!" said Zuri, standing up again.

"Then you should feel better, my dear!" said Ashti. "Honestly, Zuri. Nobody can go through Valor Dragon training and *never* lose a fight!"

"I did," said Zuri, holding her chin up. "Until yesterday, I had never once lost a fight."

"Oh, my!" said Ashti. "Is that so?"

"Yes," said Zuri.

"I see!" said Ashti. "You thought Kyra was undefeated, too. And so, when you lost your fight yesterday, you thought you had let her down. You thought she would be disappointed in you!"

Zuri nodded, and a little dragon tear escaped her eye.

Ashti took Zuri in her arms, which wasn't an easy thing to do. Ashti was quite small, and Zuri was quite large. The two hugged for a moment, and then Ashti looked Zuri in the face.

"Listen, my dear," said Ashti, "Your mother can't be with us anymore. I miss her every day. But if she could somehow see you as you train and fight, I know she'd be very proud of you no matter what."

"Thanks, Grandma," said Zuri. "That makes me feel better."

"Now," said Ashti, "let's put some ointment on those hurts and scrapes of yours. And then I will make your favorite dish for supper—roasted coal with lava sauce!"

Ashti tended to Zuri's injuries, and Zuri lay down for a nap. Ashti prepared the roasted coal and served it outside on a high cliff ledge. They ate their supper picnic style and watched the neighborhood dragons flying in the golden light of the setting sun. Zuri smiled and laughed as Ashti told stories about Kyra when she was a young dragon.

Soon the sun went down. Zuri helped Ashti collect the dishes and pans, and they went inside their cavern. Ashti warmed up two mugs of hot copper for them to drink.

"Grandma," said Zuri.

"Yes, dear?"

"Thank you for telling me more about my mom," said Zuri.

"I have many more stories I can tell you," Ashti replied with a big smile.

"Oh, that's good," Zuri replied. "I want to hear more, but I have something to do first."

"You must go back to Fire Ridge in the morning?" Ashti guessed.

"How did you know?" said Zuri.

"We've been together a long time, dearie," said Ashti. "You want to go back to prepare for your next tournament fight, don't you?"

"Yes, ma'am," said Zuri.

"I think that's what you should do, too," said Ashti. "Go and do your best, and then come back and tell me all about it."

That night, Zuri crawled into her rocky bed and thought about her mother. This time, she wasn't nervous or afraid. Then, after a short while, Zuri fell into a deep and peaceful sleep.

CHAPTER
SEVEN

It was still dark when Zuri woke up the next morning. She got out of bed quietly, so that she wouldn't wake up her grandmother.

However, when Zuri came out of her sleeping cave, she smelled the aroma of something cooking. She went to the dining cave and saw Ashti flipping flame cakes for breakfast.

"Grandma," said Zuri, "you didn't have to get up so early."

"It's no trouble," said Ashti. "I wanted you to have a nice breakfast before flying back to Fire Ridge."

"Thank you," said Zuri.

They ate breakfast, then cleaned up the dishes.

Zuri gave her grandmother a big hug, and then she flew away.

Zuri spent the next two days resting and watching tournament fights. She watched a fight between two red dragons. One of them looked familiar to Zuri.

"That's Obok!" said Zuri.

Zuri wondered what attacks Obok would use in his fight against the other red dragon. She leaned forward and waited for the fight to begin.

"When I fought Obok, he came straight at me," said Zuri to herself.

The referee waved the black flag, and the fight started. Obok immediately flew straight and low across the arena toward his opponent, whose name was Raza the Red. Obok's head was down. He meant to slam into Raza with his big horns.

Zuri felt bad for Raza. He tried to dodge to one side, but Obok was too big and fast, and Raza was slammed hard into the wall of the arena. Zuri remembered what it felt like when Obok had struck her.

"Ouch!" whispered Zuri.

Next, Obok opened his jaws and poured out his hurricane of fire. Raza was a red dragon, just like Obok, but the flames still burned him. Raza practically disappeared in the flames. He could do nothing but cover his face and eyes with his wings.

"Now Obok will fly up for one last big strike!" said Zuri.

Zuri watched, and Obok did just as she had guessed. While Raza was still recovering from Obok's breath weapon, Obok beat his mighty wings, not just to fly, but to churn up a big cloud of sand and grit.

Raza uncovered his face and looked up. He thought Obok was above him, but he wasn't. Instead, Obok swooped in and clobbered Raza from behind. It was a vicious strike, and Raza was knocked into the dust, just as Zuri had been.

"I yield!" cried Raza. He was unable to get back to his feet. The referee and Obok helped him.

"The fight is over!" shouted the referee. "Obok the Red is the winner!"

"I suppose they will invite him to be a Valor Dragon," said Zuri. "I hope I get invited, too."

Later that day, Zuri met her friend Lola in the dining cave. They ate supper and talked about their upcoming fights. Soon, they saw Master Rahu approaching.

"Hello, Zuri and Lola!" he said with a big friendly smile.

They spoke with Master Rahu for a moment, and then he said, "Both of you must go straight to the waiting caverns tomorrow after breakfast. You will be called up for your second round of fighting."

"Okay," said Zuri. "We'll be there!" She said this in a cheerful way, but she still felt anxious.

Lola and Zuri said their goodbyes and went to their sleeping caves. The hard and jagged rocks of the bed soothed Zuri's golden scales. She felt drowsy, but she couldn't fall asleep. She thought about all that had happened. She thought about her mother, Kyra, and her grandmother.

But mostly, she thought of her upcoming fight.

"If I lose tomorrow, I'll be eliminated for sure," said Zuri to herself. "I must fight perfectly tomorrow."

Then the words of Master Rahu came to her—" Just go out there and let the fight happen." Zuri also remembered the stories about Kyra that her grandmother had told her. Kyra was not a perfect fighter. She made mistakes, and she was defeated sometimes.

"Yes," Zuri whispered in the darkness. "Just let it happen. No one can be perfect all the time, and thinking about being perfect will just keep me up all night and make me groggy and afraid! I can only do my best, and let the fight happen! Of course! It's so obvious!"

This thought brought so much peace to Zuri's mind; she fell asleep only a few moments later.

In the morning, Zuri felt rested and ready to fight. She could hardly wait to get to the arena. She ate only a little breakfast and rushed to the waiting caverns.

Zuri didn't have to wait very long. Hers was one of the first names called that morning. She felt slightly nervous as she made her way through the hallway to the arena gate. It was cool and dark beneath the arena. Zuri was ready and she knew what to do.

A Valor Judge opened the gate and Zuri stepped out into the bright arena. Again, she heard the cheering of the crowd. The sand crunched beneath her paws. She looked across the arena and saw a long silver dragon—an ice dragon. There were only two blues in Zuri's clutch, so she didn't have much experience fighting them. Zuri tried not to let this worry her.

With a few wing beats, Zuri flew to the center of the arena.

"My name is Vexa the Silver!" said Zuri's opponent. He bowed his head respectfully.

"I am Zuri the Golden," said Zuri. She bowed her head to Vexa.

The referee, a large black dragon, gave them their instructions, then told them to return to their starting places.

As soon as the referee waved his black flag, Zuri

attacked. She thought she might do the same as Obok.

I can't beat Obok in a fight, thought Zuri, *but maybe I can beat someone else with his fighting ways.*

I will attack first and attack hard, thought Zuri. She took a few galloping steps, then flew into the air. In less time than it takes to blink twice, Zuri slammed into Vexa.

She had never hit another dragon with so much force!

Vexa was surprised by the strike, and he was knocked back almost to the arena wall.

Just as Obok had done, Zuri next unleashed her breath weapon. Vexa was struggling to fight back. All he could do was cover his face and eyes so that the hot gold would not blind him. Silver dragons breathe freezing wind. This may not sound so bad, but silver dragon breath can freeze an opponent solid! Zuri didn't want Vexa to get a chance to even try to use his breath weapon.

And so, Zuri spread her wings and brought them down over the sand. A great cloud of grit and dust appeared. Zuri flew up high. But unlike Obok, Zuri could not hide herself completely in the dust cloud. Vexa spotted her and blasted her with his ice wind.

There was no way Zuri could swoop around behind Vexa while he was covering her with freezing air. She could already feel herself cooling down.

"No!" muttered Zuri. "My plan is falling apart! Obok's attack isn't working for me!"

Instead of trying to strike Vexa from behind, Zuri formed several golden cannonballs in her hot dragon belly. She didn't think too much about it. She just did it.

Let it happen! she thought.

Zuri fired the heavy golden balls at Vexa. She fired them as hard as she could. One struck Vexa in the head. The next hit him in the right wing. The final shot, the strongest of the three, struck Vexa square in the chest, and knocked him onto his back.

Zuri hovered in the air above Vexa. He was hurt and could not seem to stand up. He flapped his silver wings helplessly. Zuri prepared her breath weapon.

"Do you yield, Vexa?" yelled Zuri.

"I do!" said Vexa, holding up one paw. "I yield!"

The referee shouted, "The fight is over! The winner is Zuri the Golden!"

"I did it!" whispered Zuri to herself.

"Thank you for a terrific fight!" said Vexa, struggling to his feet.

He held a paw to his head. The cannonball had made him quite dizzy.

"You have my respect, Vexa," said Zuri.

"And you have mine, Zuri," replied the silver dragon.

The crowd cheered and applauded. It had been a quick fight, but a good one. Master Rahu flew down from the stadium seats. A Valor Judge also came to the center of the arena.

"Very well done, Zuri!" said Master Rahu in his booming voice. "I see you learned a lesson from Obok!"

"Yes, Master Rahu," said Zuri. "I also learned something from you—I learned to let the fight happen without letting my thoughts get in the way."

"Good for you!" said Master Rahu.

They turned to the Valor Judge, who now stood at the center of the arena with the referee. She was a tall and elegant blue dragon.

"I am Jara, Judge of the Realm," she said. "Congratulations to you both for fighting a good fight. Vexa, you will be given three days to recover for your next fight. Zuri, you will fight again tomorrow."

Zuri was puzzled as to why she'd have to fight again, but said nothing. They bowed to Judge Jara, and then she left them.

"Are you ready for another fight," said Master Rahu as he and Zuri flew out of the arena.

"Yes, Master Rahu," said Zuri, "but I thought if I won today's fight, I would be invited to be a Valor Dragon. Why must I fight again?"

"I suppose the judges are still watching you," said Master Rahu. "There is something more they want to know about you."

Zuri went to the dining cave and ate her supper alone. Then she went to bed. She was exhausted, and she fell asleep right away and awoke feeling rested. And just like the morning before, Zuri felt ready to fight. She wasn't sure *why* she must fight again, but Master Rahu said it wasn't unusual.

"Some Small Flames have had to fight four times and even five times in the tournament," he told her.

And so, she arose and got her breakfast. She had some cinder toast and a big cup of hot copper, and then she went to a waiting cavern. After an hour or so, her name was called.

"Zuri the Golden," said the judge. "Report to the arena."

As she walked to the arena gate, she told herself she must not worry too much about the fight.

I'm a good fighter, she thought. *I can do this. Just let the fight happen. Do what is needed. Trust my training. That's all I must do.*

When she reached the arena gate, she saw Judge Jara.

"Wait here for a moment," said the tall blue dragon. "It's almost your time."

"Yes, ma'am," said Zuri.

As she waited, Zuri thought about her tournament fights. The fight with Vexa was good. The fight with Obok was not so good. What a powerful fighter he was! So large, so fast, and so strong. His horns were like steel. His breath weapon was as hot as the sun and mighty like a storm.

"It's time," said Judge Jara, opening the gate.

Zuri squinted to see her new opponent. But it wasn't a new opponent. At the other side of the arena stood Obok the Red.

EIGHT

ZURI WAS IN SHOCK AS SHE FLEW SLOWLY TO THE center of the arena. Obok bowed to her. Zuri thought he might be even bigger this time!

Obok already defeated me! thought Zuri. *How do the judges expect me to defeat him?*

Even the referee was the same slender purple dragon who had been there during Zuri's first fight.

Zuri wanted to ask if there had been some kind of mistake. However, the referees did not arrange the fights. So, there was no one to ask. Besides, Zuri knew it was not a mistake. The Valor Judges arranged the fights very carefully. They arranged the fights so that they could watch the Small Flames. Master Rahu had explained that the Valor Judges were watching for more than just fighting skill. They wanted to know if the Small Flames would fight with honor and respect.

The purple dragon referee explained the rules just as she had earlier. Obok and Zuri backed away to the edges of the arena and stood in their starting positions. Then the referee waved her black flag.

Obok was halfway across the arena before Zuri could take a breath. It was just like last time. He would charge across the arena and slam her into the wall!

Or would he?

Zuri thought, *Obok is large, fast, and powerful. But maybe not so clever. Is he really using the same attack he used on me before? Doesn't he remember me? Doesn't he realize that I know what he's doing?*

Obok came straight at her. His head was lowered, and his horns looked huge. But Zuri was not groggy that morning, and she knew exactly what Obok was doing. So, she simply jumped into the air and let Obok pass under her.

And he did! He missed Zuri completely, and then he continued—he crashed into the arena wall. In fact, he hit the wall so hard, a chip from the wall came free.

The Fire Ridge Arenas were made of the toughest steel-stone. Dragons fight hard, and so the arena must be even harder. But Obok hit the wall so hard, he left a small amount of damage.

Zuri landed gently on the arena floor. Obok stood up and staggered around. He was obviously hurt and stunned. He turned around to face Zuri.

Will he attack with his breath weapon again? thought Zuri.

He did. Obok opened his jaws and unleashed his fire. But Zuri had already moved aside, and most of the fire was unleashed harmlessly into the air.

Zuri fired her molten gold at Obok. She missed Obok during their last fight, but this time she scored a direct hit. It may not have hurt Obok very much, but it added to his dizzy confusion, and he stumbled and fell.

Now Zuri poured on her breath weapon until Obok was nearly covered in gold. When the gold cooled it became solid, and Obok was trapped.

"Do you yield, Obok?" shouted Zuri.

"No! No yield!" grumbled Obok.

Then Zuri watched in amazement as Obok stood up and shook the gold from his scales. He was truly a tough dragon fighter. Zuri did not know what to do next. How could she possibly hurt him anymore?

Obok spread his wings and quickly rose into the air. Zuri tried to keep up with him, but Obok was just too fast. When he'd risen high over the arena, he dove straight at Zuri. The massive red dragon came down from the sky just like a meteor from space. But again, Zuri was expecting Obok to charge again, and she simply moved out of the way. Obok crashed into the arena floor. The ground shook with the impact.

"Yield, Obok!" shouted Zuri. "You must yield now!"

But Obok did not answer. He was knocked out cold.

"The fight is over," cried the referee. "Obok cannot continue. The winner is Zuri the Golden!"

A cheer went up among the dragons watching from the stadium. Zuri saw Master Rahu racing straight for the center of the arena, along with Jara the Valor Judge.

It took six dragons to gently lift Obok and take him from the arena.

"Thank you for a great fight, Obok," yelled Zuri. "You have my respect."

Obok mumbled something in reply.

Master Rahu landed beside Zuri.

"Zuri, I knew you could do it!" he said, a big smile on his face.

"Did you know I was to fight Obok again?" Zuri asked.

"Yes," said Master Rahu. "But I could not tell you, of course. It would not have been fair. Do you see now what I mean? Valor Dragons cannot be just good fighters. They must have other qualities."

"Yes, Master Rahu," Zuri replied.

Judge Jara stepped forward. "Zuri the Golden, you fought well. You fought with cleverness and respect. You fought with bravery and honor. The Valor Judges invite you to become a Valor Dragon."

Zuri bowed her head. She was overcome with emotion. "Thank you, Judge Jara," she said. "I accept."

The Valor Judge presented a Valor Dragon badge and gave it to Zuri. The badge sparkled in the dusty light of the arena.

Then Judge Jara said, "Zuri, I knew Kyra the Yellow."

"You knew my mother?" asked Zuri.

"Yes," said Judge Jara. "She had much to teach me, and she was a great Valor Dragon. I am sorry she is not with us. If she were here, she would be very, very proud of you."

Zuri smiled because she knew it was true, and she couldn't wait to go home and tell Ashti all about it.

PLEASE LEAVE A REVIEW

Thank you for reading this book. I hope you enjoyed it! I would really appreciate it if you would please take a moment to review Small Flames: Zuri the Golden Dragon at the retail site where it was purchased. This helps me to reach new readers. Thank you!

—A.M. Luzzader

WWW.AMLUZZADER.COM

- blog
- freebies
- newsletter
- contact info

OTHER BOOKS BY
A.M. Luzzader

Small Flames

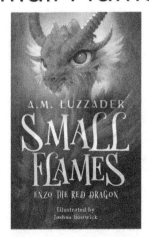

For ages
6-10

OTHER BOOKS BY
A.M. Luzzader

Decker's Video Game Rescue Agency

For ages 6-10

OTHER BOOKS BY
A.M. Luzzader

Pet Magic

For ages
6-10

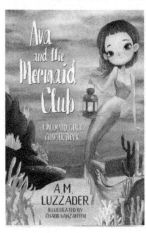 

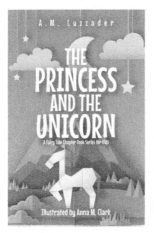
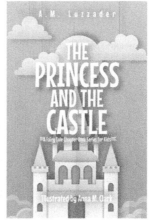

OTHER BOOKS BY
A.M. Luzzader

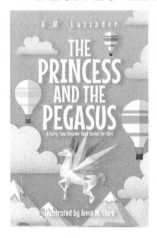 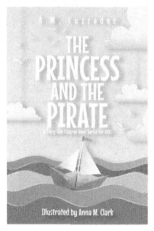

A Fairy Tale Chapter Book Series for Kids

For ages
6-10

OTHER BOOKS BY

A.M. Luzzader

Magic School for Girls

For ages
6-10

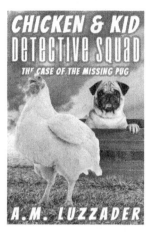 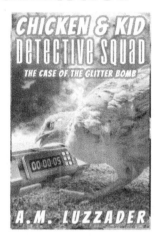

Made in United States
North Haven, CT
07 April 2024

50969884R00055